ISBN
978-1-947971-45-5
Library of Congress Control Number
2019912450
Printed in China
First Edition, 2020

25 24 23 22 21 20 5 4 3 2 1
www.LilLibros.com

www.SuperTortaBook.com | @SuperTorta.Book | SuperTorta.Book@gmail.com

Story & Art by Eric Ramos

THERE ONCE WAS A BOY
NAMED BOMBO
WHO LOVED TORTAS.

―――――――――

HABÍA UNA VEZ UN NIÑO
LLAMADO BOMBO QUE LE
ENCANTABAN LAS TORTAS.

HAM TORTAS!

CHICKEN TORTAS!

CARNE ASADA TORTAS!

BOMBO LOVED ALL TORTAS!

———————

¡TORTAS DE JAMÓN!

¡TORTAS DE POLLO!

¡TORTAS DE CARNE ASADA!

¡A BOMBO LE GUSTABAN TODAS LAS TORTAS!

ONE DAY, BOMBO HAD A
CLASS FIELD TRIP.
HE PACKED THREE TORTAS.

_____

UN DÍA, LA ESCUELA
ORGANIZÓ UNA EXCURSIÓN.
ÉL SE LLEVÓ TRES TORTAS.

SO OFF HE WENT,
ON HIS NUCLEAR POWER
PLANT FIELD TRIP.

ASÍ QUE FUE A VISITAR
UNA PLANTA NUCLEAR.

DURING THE TRIP,
ONE OF HIS TORTAS SLIPPED
OUT OF HIS LUNCH BAG.

DURANTE EL RECORRIDO,
SE LE CAYÓ UNA DE SUS
TORTAS DE LA BOLSA.

OVERNIGHT, THE TORTA
BEGAN TO GROW AND GROW...

———————

DURANTE LA NOCHE LA
TORTA COMENZÓ A CRECER
Y CRECER...

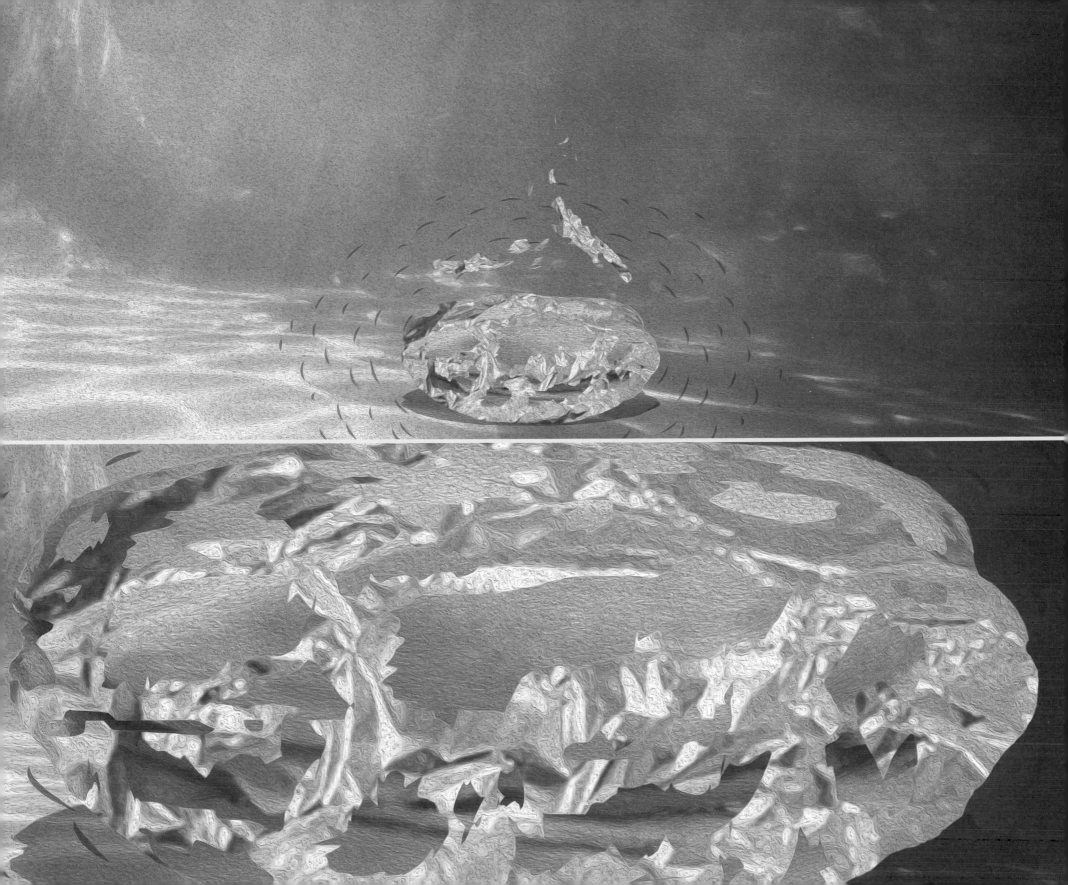

AND GROW INTO A...

_____

Y CRECIÓ HASTA
CONVERTIRSE EN UNA...

Super
TORTA!

SUPER TORTA WAS ANGRY
BECAUSE NO ONE ATE IT.

SÚPER TORTA ESTABA
ENOJADA PORQUE NADIE SE LA
HABÍA COMIDO.

SO IT JUMBLED, RUMBLED,
AND CRUMBLED
THE WHOLE CITY.

———

ASÍ QUE SACUDIÓ, RETUMBÓ,
Y DESMORONÓ
TODA LA CIUDAD.

NO ONE COULD STOP IT.
ALL HOPE WAS ABOUT
TO BE LOST!

————————

NADIE PODÍA DETENERLA.
¡HABÍAN PERDIDO
LA ESPERANZA!

LUCKY FOR US
SOMEONE CALLED BOMBO
TO THE RESCUE!

———————————

POR SUERTE PARA TODOS
¡BOMBO ACUDIÓ AL RESCATE!

WITH ONE MIGHTY BITE,
SUPER TORTA BECAME
YUMMY IN THE TUMMY.
THE WORLD CELEBRATED!

———————

LE DIO UNA MORDIDA,
Y LA SÚPER TORTA
TERMINÓ EN SU PANCITA.
¡TODO EL MUNDO LO CELEBRÓ!

THE NEXT MORNING, BACK TO
SCHOOL HE WENT WITH
HIS THREE TORTAS.

———————————

A LA MAÑANA SIGUIENTE,
DE CAMINO A LA ESCUELA BOMBO
VOLVIÓ A LLEVAR TRES TORTAS.

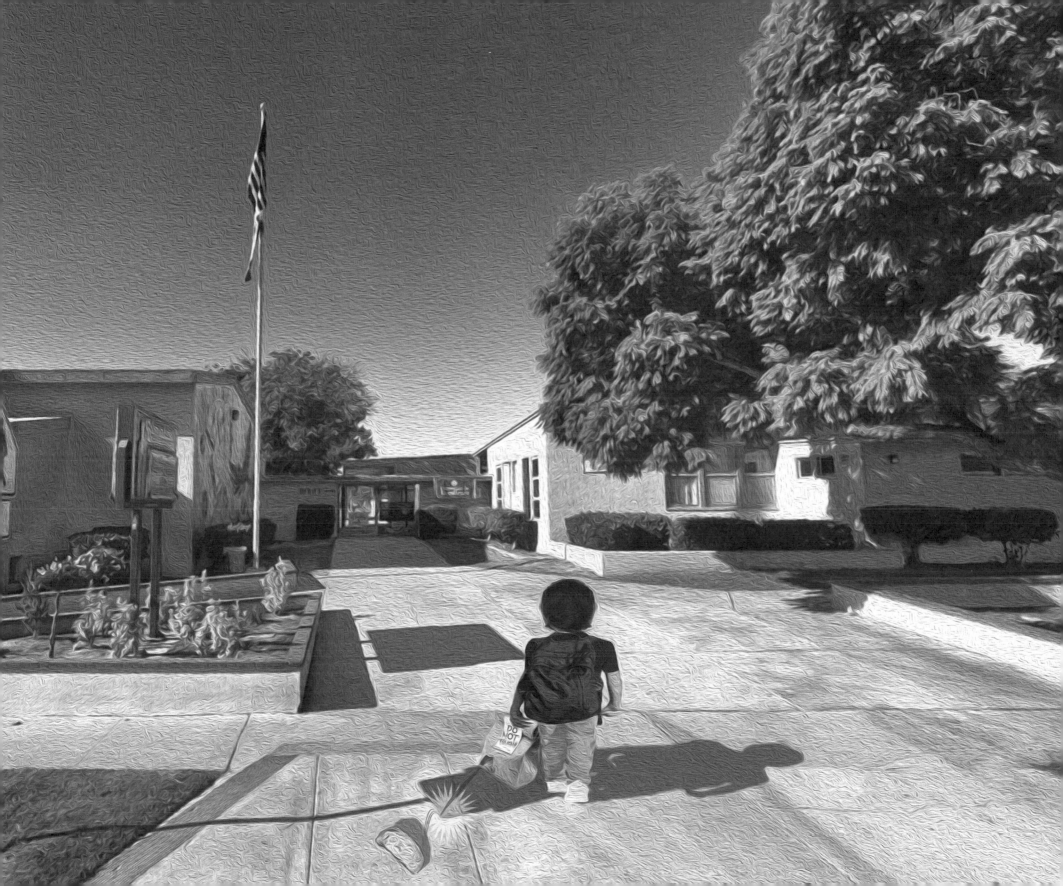

(The End)

DEDICATED TO MY MOTHER AND FATHER:
WHOSE LOVE & ATTENTION PROMOTED A LIFE OF IMAGINATION

Growing up in a predominantly Latino neighborhood on the outskirts of Los Angeles, my mother would often walk us to the library—which meant passing through a historic gang area with the unlikely name of "One Ways." Despite growing up in an environment where school shutdowns, police helicopters, and violence were commonplace, it was those library books that nurtured in us the imagination to escape the reality around us.

"Super Torta" is made up of personal memories, influences, and experiences. The story was originally written in the 7th grade as a class project. But after seeking a creative outlet from the corporate world, it was evident that such a book would find a welcome audience.

From the bottom of my heart, a special thank you to my mother who always provided my favorite meal despite a hectic schedule with 5 kids; a father who worked tirelessly to ensure a comfortable life; and to my uncles who always shared the magic of story telling.

This is my story to every neighborhood child. May they summon their imagination to change any situation, because in this world: imagination is a super power!

Gracias,
Eric Ramos
aka "Bombo"